Roommates
Again

Roommates
Again

Kathryn O. Galbraith
illustrated by Mark Graham

Margaret K. McElderry Books
NEW YORK
MAXWELL MACMILLAN CANADA
TORONTO
MAXWELL MACMILLAN INTERNATIONAL
NEW YORK OXFORD SINGAPORE SYDNEY

Once again to Steve
And to Mindy, Lisa, and Mary Jane
who shared their songs and stories with me
—K.O.G.

Margaret K. McElderry Books
Macmillan Publishing Company
866 Third Avenue
New York, NY 10022

Maxwell Macmillan Canada, Inc.
1200 Eglinton Avenue East
Suite 200
Don Mills, Ontario M3C 3N1

Macmillan Publishing Company is part of the Maxwell Communication Group of Companies.
First edition
Printed in the United States of America
10 9 8 7 6 5 4 3 2 1

Library of Congress Cataloging-in-Publication Data
Galbraith, Kathryn Osebold.
Roommates again / Kathryn O. Galbraith ; illustrated by Mark Graham — 1st ed.
p.   cm.
Summary: During their stay at Camp Sleep-Away, sisters Beth and Mimi learn some new things about each other.
ISBN 0-689-50597-3
[1. Sisters—Fiction.   2. Camps—Fiction.   3. Friendship—Fiction.]   I. Graham, Mark, date, ill.   II. Title. PZ7.G1303Rp   1994   [Fic]—dc20
93-8709

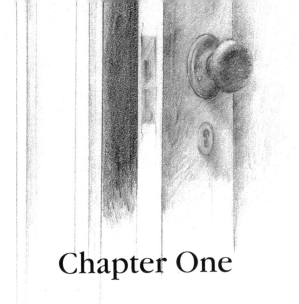

Chapter One

Beth stood outside her bedroom
door. Inside she could hear voices.

Beth shared a room with her big
sister, Mimi. They were roommates.
But who was in their room with
Mimi now?

Beth opened the door and
looked in.

There was Mimi sitting on her

own bed. Mimi's friend Kelly was sitting on Beth's bed.

Mimi and Kelly didn't look up. They didn't stop talking.

"Camp Sleep-Away is the best camp in the whole world," Kelly said. "Last summer I went swimming in the lake every day."

"Oh, I love swimming!" Mimi said.

"And every night we sang songs around the campfire."

"What kind of songs?" Beth asked.

Mimi and Kelly kept right on talking.

"What kind of songs?" Mimi asked.

"Special camp songs," Kelly

said. "You'll love them."

"Hey!" Beth said. "Hey, Mimi! Are you going away to camp?"

Mimi nodded proudly. "Kelly and I are going to Camp Sleep-Away for *four* days. It's the best camp in the whole world."

Before Beth could ask, Mimi added, "No, you can't come. Just Kelly and me. We're going to be roommates."

"Oh, who cares," said Beth. "I don't want to go to your old camp anyway." And she banged the door closed to prove it.

Then she marched out into the garden to find Mama. "How come Mimi is going to camp and I'm not?"

Mama looked surprised. "I didn't think you'd want to go. You're such a picky eater. You don't like eating away from home."

Beth frowned. She wasn't picky. She just didn't like food that was slippery or slidey. But Mama was right. She didn't want to go to camp. Not really. Not unless she could come home for breakfast, lunch, and dinner. And maybe bed-time too.

Mama gave her a hug. "I know what. While Mimi's at camp, we'll do something special together, okay?"

That night Kelly stayed for dinner. No one asked Beth what *she* wanted to do while Mimi was

gone. No one asked Beth anything.
Instead Kelly and Mimi talked
about Camp Sleep-Away.

"We have crafts every morning,"
Kelly said. "Last year we made
belts. This year I hope we make
friendship bracelets."

"I think friendship bracelets are
dumb," Beth said. But no one
seemed to hear, except her baby
sister, Rachel.

"Da," said Rachel.

"No, dumb," repeated Beth.

Beth ate the baked chicken and
her peas, but not the creamy
noodles.

"Just try them," Mama said.

Beth shivered. "Uh-uh. They're
too slippery."

Mama sighed. "Beth, you're such a picky eater."

"Picky, picky," Mimi mouthed.

Company or not, Beth reached over and pinched her.

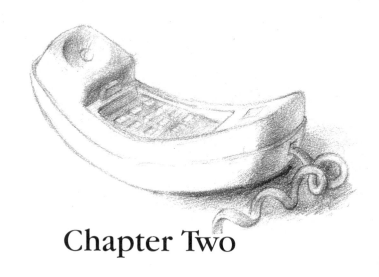

Chapter Two

Every day Kelly came over to Mimi and Beth's house. Every day she talked about Camp Sleep-Away.

Every night Mimi called Kelly on the phone. Beth sat near the phone and listened. One night Mimi said "Camp Sleep-Away" eighteen times.

Beth pretended to cover up her ears. "Mimi is so boring," she said to their dog, Willie, but she listened all the same.

On Sunday Mimi said, "Just two more days before we leave." Together Mimi and Kelly chanted, "Hooray, hooray, Camp Sleep-Away!"

On Monday Mimi said, "Just one more day!"

That's when the phone rang.

"I'll get it," Mimi said. "It's Kelly." She ran for the phone.

It was Kelly, but something was wrong.

Mimi's mouth made a big round O. "Oh, no!"

Mimi ran into the kitchen. "Mama, guess what!"

Beth couldn't wait to hear. She ran into the kitchen, too.

"Kelly has the chicken pox!" Mimi said. "She can't go to camp!"

"Oh, poor Kelly," Mama said. "But don't worry, Mimi. You can still go. You and Beth have already had the chicken pox."

Mimi looked at Mama. "Go to camp alone? All by myself?"

Mimi was very quiet all day long. She was very quiet and very nice to Beth. She didn't even tease Beth about leaving all of her spaghetti on her plate.

That night she said, "Hey, Beth. You can come to camp if you want to."

"Me?" Beth looked up in surprise.

"Sure. We'll be roommates."

Beth thought about going to camp. She thought about the lake and the campfires and the songs. Then she thought about eating breakfast, lunch, and dinner at camp for four whole days. She shook her head. At Camp Sleep-Away they probably had spaghetti every single day.

"Come on, Beth, please. It will be fun."

Mimi didn't say please very often. But Beth just shook her head harder.

"Please, Beth." Mimi began to tickle her. "Please, please, please!"

Beth tried to twist away. "No, Mimi, stop!"

But Mimi wouldn't stop. "Come on, Beth. Say yes. Yes, yes, yes!"

"Mimi, stop, stop!" Beth shrieked. "Okay, okay, yes!" The word just slipped out.

"Hooray!" Mimi began bouncing up and down on her bed. "Hooray, hooray, Camp Sleep-Away!"

Mimi chanted all by herself. Suddenly Beth's throat felt dry. Her stomach felt empty. Now she wished she'd never heard of Camp Sleep-Away. Now she wished she had never even heard of Mimi.

carry their packs and sleeping bags down the path.

The Daisy cabin was small and neat. There were just two sets of bunk beds and one small closet. One set of bunk beds had sleeping bags on them already.

"I'll take this top bunk," Mimi said quickly. She looked at Beth. "I saw it first."

Beth put her sleeping bag on the lower bunk. Let Mimi sleep up in the air. She was glad to take this bottom one.

Goooonnnng! rang a big, deep bell.

"Oh, good," Libby said. "Dinner! I'm starved."

Beth and Mimi were hungry, too.

They followed Libby to the picnic tables under the trees. Libby introduced them to the long row of faces.

"Katie and Allison are in the Daisy cabin, too," Libby said. "You're all roommates."

Katie and Allison smiled at them. Beth and Mimi smiled back.

Then Beth looked down at her plate. "Oh, yuck!" It was covered with slippery, slidey spaghetti and lots of red gooey sauce.

"Beth, you shouldn't be so picky," Mimi said. "You should be like me." She raised her voice. "*I'm* not picky about anything."

Beth glared at Mimi. She wasn't picky either! She just didn't like spaghetti. Besides, it was all Mimi's fault she was here at all. Mimi should be nice to her. Mimi should say, "Poor Beth, poor hungry Beth."

Instead Mimi said, "If you don't want it, can I have your spaghetti too?"

Without waiting for an answer, Mimi slid all of Beth's spaghetti onto her plate.

Beth pushed her plate away. Now she didn't have any dinner at all. Now she was going to starve. And it was all Mimi's fault. Mimi and her dumb Camp Sleep-Away.

Suddenly someone said, "Oh, poor Beth!" It was Libby. "You didn't have anything to eat. Do you want a peanut butter sandwich?"

Libby pointed to the end table. There next to the giant pot of spaghetti was a giant stack of bread. And next to the bread was a huge jar of peanut butter and one of jam.

"Peanut butter and jam are put out for every meal," Libby said.

Beth hurried over to the table. She made two peanut butter sand-wiches. Then she sat down next to Mimi. She took a big bite. *"Mmmm."* It was the best sandwich she had ever eaten.

"I love peanut butter, too," Alli-son said.

Beth smiled. Maybe, just maybe, Camp Sleep-Away wasn't going to be so bad after all.

Mimi gave her a poke. "You should have eaten your spaghetti like *I* did. Besides, peanut butter is slippery, too."

"No, it'th not," Beth said. She started to giggle. It was hard to talk with her mouth full of peanut butter. "Peanut butter'th great. It thstickth to everything!"

Chapter Four

After dinner, everyone gathered around the campfire.

Libby taught them a funny song about Sara the whale. Then they sang one about a bear in tennis shoes.

Mimi and Beth giggled. Libby winked at them in the firelight. Beth was glad she was in Libby's cabin. Libby was so nice.

When the fire began to die down, Libby taught them the good-night song. Everyone linked arms and sang,

"Camp Sleep-Away forever,
We love you true and blue.
Camp Sleep-Away forever,
We'll always remember you."

As the voices faded into the night sky, Libby said, "Bedtime."

Beth and Mimi walked back to their cabin with Katie and Allison. They unrolled their sleeping bags and shook out their pillows. Then they made one last trip down the long, dark path to the bathroom and back.

Libby poked her head in the doorway. "Good night, Daisies. And remember, I'll be right next door if you need me. Now sleep tight and don't let the bedbugs bite." She turned out the light and closed the door.

Suddenly the cabin was dark. Pitch-dark. Mimi carefully rolled over in her bunk. The bunk seemed very high. The ceiling seemed very low. She knew there weren't any bedbugs, but. . . .

Mimi's heart began to thump. But what if there were spiders crawling on the ceiling? Ugh, she hated spiders. Then she had a worse thought. What if there were spiders and one fell down on her!

Mimi shivered. She pulled the edge of the sleeping bag over her face. Now she wished she was in her own bed. Her nice low bed at home.

"Good night," Mimi heard Katie whisper. "Good night, good night," she heard Allison and Beth answer.

After a few giggles, the cabin grew quiet. Mimi squeezed her eyes shut. She tried to sleep, but she couldn't. Not with the spiders right over her head.

Long, slow minutes passed. It felt like midnight. Suddenly Mimi had another terrible thought. What if she had to go to the bathroom? What if she had to slip past the spiders and walk down that long path by herself? In the dark. In the pitch-dark.

Mimi was sorry she'd thought of going to the bathroom. Now she did have to go. She had to go right now, spiders or not.

There wasn't a sound in the cabin. Everyone seemed to be asleep.

Slowly, Mimi inched out of her sleeping bag. Then she slipped over the side of the bed and jumped to the floor.

"*Psssst*, Beth, wake up. Do you have to go to the bathroom?"

"No, uh-uh." Beth sounded very sleepy.

"Yes, you do," Mimi whispered.

She unzipped Beth's sleeping bag.
"Come on. I'll go with you."

Beth leaned against Mimi and
yawned. She pushed her feet into
her rubber flip-flops.

"Wait," Mimi whispered. She felt
around the floor. She found her
sneakers and put them on. There
might be crickets in the bathroom.
Or beetles. She tied her shoes with

26

a double knot. She didn't want anything running across *her* toes.

Outside, Beth was wide awake. She tipped her head back. "Oh, look at the stars. They're shining through the treetops."

Mimi didn't look at the stars. She tried to watch her feet instead. Were there grasshoppers in the woods? Or big furry moths? Mimi walked a little faster.

In the cold damp bathroom, there were shadows and—

Mimi's toes curled up in her sneakers.

"Oh, yuck! There's a cricket."

"Well, chase it away," Beth said.

Mimi gasped again. "Look, a spider. A big one!"

Mimi heard Beth make a choking sound. Was Beth crying? Was she scared, too? Mimi whirled around.

No, Beth was laughing. Beth was laughing at her!

"It's not funny," Mimi said. "I hate spiders! I hate bugs!"

Beth giggled louder. "Picky, picky," she sang.

Chapter Five

The next morning Mimi was very quiet. Quiet and worried. What if Beth told Katie and Allison about last night? What if she told Libby too? They'd think she was a baby. A great big baby.

"Good morning, Daisies," Libby called. She pushed open the cabin door. "How did you girls sleep?"

"Fine!" said Katie and Allison.

Mimi held her breath. What would Beth say?

Beth looked at Mimi and giggled. "Fine," she said. "Just fine."

At breakfast they were served big bowls of oatmeal. Beth made herself a big peanut butter sandwich instead.

"Don't you like oatmeal?" Katie asked. She offered Beth a spoonful. "Here, try it."

"Uh-uh." Beth shook her head. "It wiggles."

"Wiggles!" Katie started to laugh.

Beth felt her face grow hot. "It's not funny," she wanted to say.

But then suddenly Mimi said it for her.

"It's not funny," Mimi said.

"Everybody's picky about something."

Beth looked at Mimi in surprise.
Then she smiled. For once, just
once, Mimi was right.

After breakfast, it was craft time.

"Look what we're going to
make," Libby said. "Friendship
bracelets."

Beth looked at Libby's soft,
woven bracelet. It was made out
of blue and yellow and white
embroidery thread. She forgot
that friendship bracelets were
dumb.

"Oh," she said. "It's so pretty."

Libby smiled. "It's special, too,"
she said, "because you make it for a
special friend."

Libby showed them how to cut the strands of thread. She showed them how to knot the strands together.

"Now," Libby said, "look in the craft box and choose three colors."

Beth was first. Her favorite color was pink. She picked out three shades of pink for her bracelet.

Then it was Mimi's turn. Beth peeked over Mimi's shoulder. "What colors did you pick out?"

Mimi hid her embroidery thread behind her back. "It's a surprise," she said. "I'm making my bracelet for Kelly."

"Then you can't see mine either," Beth said. "I'm making mine for my friend Heather."

Mimi and Beth worked on their bracelets all morning.

For lunch Mimi ate a big slice of pizza. Beth ate a peanut butter sandwich.

In the afternoon, everyone went swimming. The sun was hot, but—"*Brrrr!* The water's cold," yelled Allison and Katie.

Beth and Mimi held hands and jumped in after them. "It's not cold," they shrieked. "It's freeeeeezing!"

Mimi ate creamed chipped beef on toast for dinner. "*Mmmm,* good," she said.

Beth ate her toast with peanut butter. "*Mmmm,* delicious!"

After dinner, the whole camp

played a game of Cat and Mice. Mimi was the cat. She giggled so hard, she got the hiccups.

That night Mimi said, "Just two more days left." She sighed. "I wish we could stay here forever."

Then she thought about the crickets in the bathroom. She thought about the spiders on the ceiling. "Well, almost forever," she said.

The next day was Friday. In the afternoon, Libby took everyone on a nature hike. After dinner, they played Pom-Pom Pullaway. Then they played Sardines. That was Beth's favorite.

That night Beth said, "Just one more day left." She sighed. She *almost* wished she could stay at camp forever, too.

On the last night, they had a singing contest, each cabin against the others. The Rose cabin won first prize for knowing the most songs. The Daisy cabin won first prize for singing the loudest.

"You know what?" Beth whispered to Mimi. "Camp Sleep-Away is the best camp in the whole world."

"No, it's not," Mimi said.

Beth looked surprised. "It's not?"

"No," Mimi said. "It's the best camp in the whole *wide* world."

Chapter Six

Beth and Mimi looked out the car window.

WELCOME HOME! said the big sign on the front lawn.

"Hooray, we're home," Beth and Mimi cried.

As Mama stopped the car, Daddy came out the front door. In his arms was baby Rachel. "Da!" cried Rachel.

Right behind Daddy and Rachel came Grandpa Jack. Then out dashed Willie. He ran around in circles and barked.

Beth and Mimi gave everyone a hug. Then they caught Willie and hugged him too.

Mimi and Beth talked all about Camp Sleep-Away. They talked about Libby and Katie and Allison. They talked about playing Cat and Mice. They talked about swimming in the cold, cold lake.

Finally Grandpa Jack covered his ears. "You've said 'Camp Sleep-Away' at least eighteen times," he teased.

But Beth and Mimi didn't stop.

Mimi talked about sleeping every night in the top bunk, but . . . she

didn't tell about the spiders on the
ceiling. Or the crickets in the bathroom.

　　She waited. Beth didn't tell
about them either.

　　Beth talked about the picnic
tables under the trees, but . . . she

didn't tell about the peanut butter sandwiches. The peanut butter sandwiches for breakfast, lunch, and dinner.

She waited. Mimi didn't tell about them either.

That night they all had a picnic in the backyard.

Beth ate the green beans and the barbecued chicken. She ate the cherries out of the cherry pie, too, but not the gooey cherry sauce.

Mama sighed. "I see some things never change."

After dinner, Beth and Mimi sang camp songs. They sang and sang until Rachel fell asleep in Daddy's lap.

"Bedtime," Mama said.

Mimi and Beth put on their nightgowns. Beth wiggled her bare toes. "No crickets," she said.

Mimi laughed. "No spiders either."

Mimi climbed into her bed. Her nice low bed.

Beth climbed into her own bed. "Mimi," she whispered. She hugged her knees and giggled. "Look under your pillow."

Slowly, slowly, Mimi lifted the edge of her pillow. "A friendship bracelet! I thought you made it for Heather."

Beth shook her head. "No, I made it for you. And see, it's pink. My favorite color."

Mimi laughed. "Now look under *your* pillow," she said.

42

Beth's fingers touched something soft. "Oh, a friendship bracelet!" She held it up. "And it's pink!"

"I know," Mimi said. "It's your favorite color."

Mimi helped Beth tie on her bracelet. Beth helped Mimi tie hers on too. Then they rubbed their wrists together three times.

"Now we're friends forever," Mimi said.

Then softly they sang,

"Camp Sleep-Away forever,
We love you true and blue.
Camp Sleep-Away forever,
We'll always remember you."